WITHDRAWN

Michael Le Soufflé
and the
APRIL FOOL

Michael Le Soufflé
and the
APRIL FOOL

Written and Illustrated by
Peter J. Welling

PELICAN PUBLISHING COMPANY

Gretna 2003

To the folks who got me this far: Darlene and my family;
my former agent, Kay Lewis "Happy" Shaw;
my critique group—Trish Batey, Carol Katterjohn, and Sara Murray-Plumer;
my publisher and the crew at Pelican;
and to Kristine Von Ogden, who provided the French translations, merci beaucoup.

The word "Pelican" and the depiction of a pelican are trademarks
of Pelican Publishing Company, Inc., and are registered
in the U.S. Patent and Trademark Office.

Library of Congress Cataloging-in-Publication Data

Welling, Peter J.
   Michael le Soufflé and the April Fool / written and illustrated by Peter J. Welling.
      p. cm.
   Summary: In the small town of Bakonnegss, France, the grumpy mayor, a pig named
Melon de Plume, and a happy red rooster, Michael le Soufflé, battle wits until they
learn to enjoy April Fools' Day together. Includes glossary of French vocabulary.
   ISBN 1-58980-105-9 (alk. paper)
   [1. Pigs—Fiction. 2. Roosters—Fiction. 3. April Fools' Day—Fiction. 4. Humorous
stories. 5. French language—Vocabulary.] I. Title.

PZ7.W4573 Mi 2003
[Fic]—dc21

                                              2002013505

Printed in China

Published by Pelican Publishing Company, Inc.
1000 Burmaster Street, Gretna, Louisiana 70053

Michael Le Soufflé
and the April Fool

The legend of the April fool began long ago in the small town of Bakonneggs, France. On Bon Temps Street lived Michael Le Soufflé, a happy rooster. Across the street lived the mayor, Melon de Plume, a grouchy pig.

Michael laughed, "Cock-ha-ha-ha-doodle-doo," when he played jokes on folks, especially if it was the mayor.

The mayor, a lumpy, grumpy hog, didn't think any-thing was funny. When Michael started each day with a laugh, Melon would pull his downy pillow over his big pig ears and groan, "What could be so humorous so early in the day?"

One morning, over a breakfast of sour grapes, lemon rinds, and dill pickles, Melon said, "I will make laughing illegal. That should shut that dumb cluck up."

He nailed the law to the council oak tree.
"Oh no," Michael clucked. "This will never cock-
a-doodle-do."

"Ring the emergency bell," Michael said.
CLONG BONG!

Everyone gathered on the green. "The mayor declared that it is illegal to laugh," Michael said. Then he sang, juggled, and danced a little jig. Everyone laughed.

"Stop laughing," Melon de Plume said, "or you'll be arrested."

Michael laughed, "Cock-ha-doodle-doo-doo-DOO!"
Everyone laughed even louder.

"Police!" the mayor screamed.

Within minutes, the jail cells were full, and the stocks were full, but people were still outside laughing. "Nevermind," Melon sighed. "Let them out."

Melon spent the next day fishing. He came home with a load of fish and walked inside. "Squeeeeeal!" he cried. "Someone's been messing with my things!"

"There's no dust. There are no cobwebs. They've even put fresh straw in my bed. What a dastardly thing to do," Melon grumped.

In the morning, Melon took his pig pen and wrote a new law.

"It is illegal to be neat and clean," it said. "Everyone must live in a pigsty." Melon grinned. "That should fix Monsieur Michael Le Soufflé's cheese. Nail it to the tree," he told one of his creatures.

Melon barely settled his large behind behind his desk when there arose such a clatterbang clanging that he scraped his pig knuckles rushing to see what the commotion was. A bucket brigade was cleaning everything as they marched. Ahead of them all strutted Michael Le Soufflé.

"Clean-a-doodle-doodle-doo," he said.

"Stupid chicken," Melon grumbled as he took down the new law.

"Cock-ha-ha-ha-doodle-doo. Can't you laugh or give us a little piggy giggle, mayor?"

"Go lay an egg," Melon said. "I've written another law that should tickle your fancy. It says no feathers are allowed in town."

Michael shook his head. "That means all the birds would have to leave," he said. "And you'll have to pull the plumes from your hats and dump your downy pillow."

DOWNY PILLOWS

UNE CORBEAU

Melon sighed. He didn't care if the silly birds left, but his beautiful hats and oh-so-soft pillow had to stay. He shredded the law and went home.

"Bring me some slop," Melon bellowed. "Bring me swill." He filled his glass from the pork barrel. His creepy friends fetched his dinner. "I must get rid of that cavalier rooster."

Melon heard a noisy crowd in the streets.
"Now what?" he groaned. There was a rooster posting something to the council oak. "What do you think you're doing?" he sputtered, but no one heard him. He rushed outside.

The crowd moved on, singing, dancing, and following the rooster. Melon read the notice: "Attention all Frenchmen, by order of the king of France, New Year's Day will no longer be celebrated on April 1. Next year, we will start celebrating it on January 1, the King."

Melon couldn't believe it. Grabbing a peddler's fish cart, he hurled fish at the rooster as he chased after him. "Your silly jokes have gone too far," Melon yelled. "Only the king and I can post new laws!"

"Cock-a-doodle-boo-boo," Michael crowed. "Never throw fish at the king." Michael was standing under a tree. The king of France was standing under a pile of fish.

"Oh no," Melon bawled.

Melon's hog jowls started jiggling, "Y-y-your majesty, I didn't know it was you. I thought it was another goofy rooster. I mean, changing New Year's Day to January 1 is a joke, right? No one but a fool would try to change the calendar."

"Fool?" the king screeched. "Aaawk! Listen, piggy, my buddy the Easter Bunny said Easter came too soon or too late. My friend Gregory the Papal Bull fixed things by erasing ten days from the calendar. Now, I get my jellybeans on time." The king frowned. "As for doing silly things, throwing fish at me wasn't very smart. How would *you* like to be smacked by a mackerel?

"Now, don't lose your head, your highness," Melon said.

All the king's men grabbed Melon and put him in the stocks. Everyone tossed tuna and trout at him until Melon was covered in fish.

"We shall call this day April Fish Day," the king said.

"April Fools' Day would be better," the papal bull whispered. For years thereafter, Melon again wished everyone happy new year on April 1. The king always ordered that the stubborn pig be flogged with fish.

"What a fool Melon de Plume is," Michael laughed. "Or is he? I think something is fishy. After the fish fly, I think I will stick around to see what's up."

Michael hid in a bucket. When everyone was gone, Melon shoveled all the fish into his cart and waddled home.

That night, the pig threw his annual Melon Ball. He and his friends took rides in hot-air balloons. That was the first time anyone saw a pig fly. Melon de Plume did a few piggy-jigs and sang "Auld Lang Swine" and they all ate fish until they were full and then some.

Michael Le Soufflé popped out of the shadows, "Cock-a-doodle-doodle-doo, we thought we pulled a joke on you."

Melon shook his head. "It didn't turn out that way. The joke's on you this April Fools' Day!" Then, Melon de Plume laughed.

Melon and Michael became good friends. They joked, laughed, and told everyone about April Fools' Day. Melon even wrote a little song about it.

"Let's sing it for the king," Melon said. So they did.

"On April Fools' Day, have lots of fun
By playing tricks on everyone.
But make sure you know your audience,
Never throw fish at the king of France."

GLOSSARY

Agneau:	(an-yO) Sheep
Banane:	(ba-non) Banana
Bœuf:	(buf) Ox
Castor:	(ka-store) Beaver
Chat:	(sha) Cat
Chêne:	(shen) Oak tree
Cochon:	(kO-shohn) Pig
Coco-ri-co:	(kO-kO-rE-kO) Cock-a-doodle-doo
Coiffures:	(kwafewr) Hairstyles
Coq:	(cuck) Rooster
Corbeau:	(core-bOw) Crow
Cordonnerie:	(kor-done-ree) Cobbler
Crapaud:	(kra-pO) Toad
Crémerie:	(krem-ree) Dairy store
Éléphant:	(el-A-fahn) Elephant
Épicerie:	(A-pis-ree) Small grocery store
Escargot:	(ess-car-gO) Snail
Fromage:	(frO-maj) Cheese
Gargouille:	(gar-goo-yuh) Gargoyle
Grenouille:	(gruh-noo-yuh) Frog

Hamster:	(am-stair)	Hamster
Hippopotame:	(ee-pO-pah-tam)	Hippopotamus
Marmotte:	(mar-mutt)	Groundhog
Oiseau rouge:	(whazo -rooj)	Red bird
Ombre:	(Ome-bruh)	Shadow
Orange:	(oar-onge)	Orange
Poire:	(pware)	Pear
Poisson:	(pwah-sohn)	Fish
Pomme:	(pum)	Apple
Raton laveur:	(rah-tohn la-vur)	Raccoon
Renard:	(ruh-nar)	Fox
Serpent:	(sair-pahn)	Snake
Souris:	(soo-rE)	Mouse
Tarte:	(tart)	pie
Vache:	(vash)	cow
Ver:	(vair)	Worm

Cock-a-doodle-*adieu* (farewell)!

COCK-A-DOODLE ADIEU.